BUDDY AND BEA
Pet-a-Palooza

To Gwen Agna, wise and kind principal, who brought Jackson the therapy dog to Jackson Street School. And to Gwen's daughters, Nell and Kate, and *their* daughters, Esme and Franny.

—J.C.

For George, baby Harper, and for my dad.

—K.M.

Published by
PEACHTREE PUBLISHING COMPANY INC.
1700 Chattahoochee Avenue
Atlanta, Georgia 30318-2112
PeachtreeBooks.com

Text © 2024 by Jan Carr
Illustrations © 2024 by Kris Mukai

All rights reserved. No part of this publication may be reproduced, stored in a retrieval system, or transmitted in any form or by any means—electronic, mechanical, photocopy, recording, or any other—except for brief quotations in printed reviews, without the prior permission of the publisher.

Edited by Catherine Frank
Design and composition by Lily Steele
The illustrations were rendered digitally.

Printed and bound in January 2024 at Lake Book Manufacturing,
Melrose Park, IL, USA
10 9 8 7 6 5 4 3 2 1
First Edition
ISBN: 978-1-68263-536-0

Cataloging-in-Publication Data is available from the Library of Congress.

BUDDY AND BEA
Pet-a-Palooza

Jan Carr
Illustrated by Kris Mukai

PEACHTREE
ATLANTA

CONTENTS

CHAPTER ONE: A Different Kind of Treat

CHAPTER TWO: Pet Party

CHAPTER THREE: Booky

CHAPTER FOUR: Herding Cats

CHAPTER FIVE: Training Frisbee

CHAPTER SIX: Fuzzy

CHAPTER SEVEN: Fibber

CHAPTER EIGHT: Dog for a Day

CHAPTER NINE: Bodega Cat

CHAPTER ONE
A Different Kind of Treat

One morning, Buddy noticed a stack of notebooks in his classroom. They were on a shelf near the book baskets. In second grade, they used a lot of notebooks. One for math. And one for science. But these notebooks just had their names on them. Nothing more.

Buddy looked at Joey, his best friend. "Where did these come from?" he asked.

Bea walked over to join them. She always stuck her nose in whatever Buddy was doing. She tried to pick up the whole stack. "*Oof!*" she said. "These guys are heavy. What are they for?"

Buddy shrugged.

"You mean, it's a *mystery*?" said Bea. She waggled her eyebrows, like she was trying to look mysterious. But to Buddy, she just looked goofy.

"A *Whirligigs* mystery," said Joey.

Whirligigs was the name of their class. Because whirligigs were maple seeds. And their teacher's name was Ms. Maple.

Ms. Maple overheard them. "No mystery," she said. "Those are your writers' notebooks. I got them out since we're about to start working in them. And to celebrate, I've planned a surprise." She smiled. Mysteriously!

"Is it cake?" asked Bea.

"No," said Ms. Maple.

"Pizza?" asked Buddy.

Ms. Maple shook her head. "Not food," she said. "It's a different kind of treat."

All the Whirligigs crowded around.

"We're going to have an *author visit*!" said Ms. Maple.

Oh. Buddy drooped. That was disappointing.

"What's an author visit?" asked Bea.

"We had one last year," said Joey.

"Yeah," said Bea. "But I didn't go to this school last year. Remember?"

"It's when an author comes to our school," said Buddy. "And we have to go to the auditorium to see them. Last year we were supposed to sit in front 'cause we're still short. But we got there late. So the big kids had already taken our seats. And we had to sit in back. None of us could see anything. At all!"

"Oh dear," said Ms. Maple. "I'm sorry that happened to you."

"And we had a whole bunch of questions for the author," said Buddy. "'Cause we'd read every book of hers. I waved my hand like crazy, but she couldn't see me. She never called on any of us!"

Bea made a sour face. Like sucking on a lemon. "Author visits sound *terrible*," she said.

"Well," said Ms. Maple. "That one doesn't sound like it was the best experience."

"It doesn't sound like a *treat*," said Bea. "You know what would be a treat? Cake. Like I suggested."

"Or pizza," said Malik.

"Or both!" said Omar.

"Whirligigs," said Ms. Maple. The class quieted. They liked their name. And they liked to hear Ms. Maple say it. "I've already scheduled our author visit. For later in the week."

Everyone groaned.

"But," said Ms. Maple, "I think this one will be a lot more fun." She waved them over to the rug. She held up some books she had there.

"Picture books?" said Malik. "Those are for kindergarteners!"

"Oh no," said Ms. Maple. "Picture books can be quite sophisticated. We'll be reading lots this year. Has anyone read these?"

No one had.

Tamar read the author's name on the covers. "Roxy Fox." She made a face. "That doesn't even sound like a real name. Is it a *pen name*?" Tamar knew everything about books. Her dad was a librarian. But Buddy knew about pen names, too. They were made-up names for authors. That sometimes authors used for their books.

"Actually," said Ms. Maple, "Roxy Fox is her real name. And she's a friend of mine. We've planned a cozy visit. Here in our classroom, not the big auditorium."

"Just us Whirligigs?" asked Kaveh.

"Just us Whirligigs." Ms. Maple lined up the books. "Before she visits, we'll come up with questions to ask. And observations."

"All her books look different," said Marisol.

"Ah," said Ms. Maple. "And why do you think that is?"

"*Ooh! Ooh!*" said Tamar. "I know! Because all the *illustrators* are different!"

"Exactly," said Ms. Maple. "Roxy's an author. Not an illustrator. Some authors do both. But Roxy has a different illustrator for each book."

Ms. Maple opened the first book and started to read.

Buddy sat up straighter. He wanted to listen carefully. So he could come up with a good question. Maybe, this time, the author would call on him.

And Buddy wanted to have the best question of all.

CHAPTER TWO
Pet Party

On the day Roxy Fox came to visit, the Whirligigs were ready. They had a lot of things to say about her books. And they couldn't wait to tell her! As soon as they settled on the rug, Buddy's hand shot up high. But Roxy Fox wanted to read to them first.

"You don't *need* to," said Bea. "We already read your books."

"True," said Ms. Maple. "But it will be fun to hear Roxy read. That way, when you read her books on your own, you'll hear her voice in your heads."

"Her *voice*?" said Bea. "You mean like *earbuds*?"

Buddy put his hand back in his lap. It didn't seem polite to keep it up while Roxy Fox was reading. But as soon as she finished, he raised it again. She didn't call on him, though. The girls were all sitting in front, and they called out quickly, rat-a-tat.

"One thing we noticed," said Priya, "is that all your books are fiction."

"And you use a lot of poetic language," said Keiko. "Even though they're not poems exactly."

"And all your books have different illustrators," said Tamar.

"Because you're *only* an author!" said Bea. "*Not* an illustrator, too. So I need to talk to you about that. Because when *I* write a story, I do the pictures myself. You should learn to draw. Like me!"

Roxy Fox laughed. "The truth is," she said, "I'm not a very good artist."

"Ooooh," said Bea. "*Don't* say that." Her voice sounded fake and sing-song-y. Like she was trying too hard to be encouraging. "I bet you're *really* good. Let's see you draw something."

"Right now?" asked Roxy Fox.

"Go ahead," said Bea. "*Try.*"

Roxy Fox uncapped a marker. She drew on the big pad of paper.

"Is that a person?" asked Bea, squinting.

"It's supposed to be a bunny," said Roxy Fox. "See? I told you I wasn't very good."

"*Oh nooooo*," said Bea. "It's a really *good* bunny. Isn't it, Whirligigs? Roxy Fox, you keep trying. If you try hard, you'll get better."

Buddy was getting impatient. Was this visit going to be like last year? When the author didn't even call on him?

Roxy Fox pointed in his direction. "Yes?" she said.

Buddy froze. Did she mean him?

"You," she said. "The student with the snazzy glasses."

Buddy pushed his glasses higher on his nose. And then he forgot what he was going to say.

"Um," he said. He stalled for time. "What *I* noticed . . ." Oh! He remembered! "Is that there are *dogs* in all your books. Every one. So my question is: Why?"

"Dogs?" said Roxy Fox. She looked surprised. "There are?"

"In the pictures," said Buddy.

Roxy Fox opened her books and looked, one by one. Buddy was right. Each book had a dog. Different dogs, but there they were. In the art. In the backgrounds.

"Interesting," said Roxy Fox. "I never mention a dog in the stories."

"Do you have a dog?" asked Joey.

"I don't," said Roxy Fox.

"Do you have *any* pets?" asked Marisol.

She didn't.

"Do the *illustrators* have dogs?" asked Tamar.

"Well," said Roxy Fox. "I'm guessing they do. Maybe they wanted to include their pets in the pictures. What do you think?"

Joey raised his hand. "I have a new puppy," he said. "Her name is Frisbee. She likes to sit on my lap. And I give her rides in my wheelchair."

Buddy chimed in. "I have a cat. Her name is Sunshine. Which isn't really a good name for her. Because she bites and scratches."

"My cat knocks everything off the table," said Marisol.

"My guinea pig keeps me awake at night," said Malik.

"I won my goldfish at the school fair," said Tamar.

Roxy Fox looked a bit startled. "You all have a lot to say about your pets!"

Ms. Maple laughed. "Welcome to the World of Whirligigs!" she said. "My students have their own ideas. And, often, their own agenda."

"We like to whirl things up together!" said Bea.

"You definitely do," said Ms. Maple. "But let's talk about writers' notebooks. Since we're about to start working in them."

"Ah," said Roxy Fox. "I'll show you mine." She held up a notebook. "Do you know why I call this my writer's notebook?"

Was that a trick question? It seemed pretty obvious.

"Because you're a writer?" said Tamar.

"Yes," said Roxy Fox. "But it's my writer's *notebook* because I write *notes* in it. Observations. Snippets. Anything I want! Things that aren't stories yet but might grow into them." She picked up a marker and started a list on the big pad.

- Interesting words or bits of language
- Descriptions of people or nature
- Snatches of conversation I overhear on the street

"You mean you *eavesdrop*?" asked Priya.

"I guess I do," said Roxy Fox.

"That's not polite," said Bea. "My gran said!"

"It's not polite to *spy*," said Roxy Fox. "But sometimes, we just overhear conversations. And that can help us understand people, how they think and talk. So we can create good characters."

Ms. Maple rubbed her hands together like she was hatching a plan. "These are all good ideas for our writers' notebooks. Right, Whirligigs?"

"Yeah," said Malik. "We could eavesdrop on our *pets*. My guinea pig, Rocket, makes weird noises. Like squeaks. And whistles. He sounds like an alien landing!"

"Pets again!" said Roxy Fox. She added the word to her list.

• Pets

She smiled at the class. "It feels like we're having a pet party here."

"A Pet-a-Palooza!" said Ms. Maple.

Soon it was time for Roxy Fox to leave.

"It was good to meet you," said Bea. "Even though you're just an author. Maybe you should invite me to your house to do an *illustrator* visit. I could teach you how to draw."

"I'm sure you could," said Roxy Fox. She looked at Buddy. "And thank *you* for pointing out the dogs in the art. Your question started the whole pet discussion."

Buddy grinned. It had!

He'd started the Pet-a-Palooza!

CHAPTER THREE
Booky

That afternoon, the whole class wrote thank-you notes to Roxy Fox. Everyone had something they wanted to say.

"I'm sorry you don't have a dog," wrote Joey.

"You must be really lonely without a pet," wrote Marisol.

"Are you allergic to pet dander?" wrote Tamar. "Then you could get a goldfish, like me."

"Don't forget to practice your drawing!" wrote Bea. "Because if you don't practice, you won't get better!"

After the thank-you notes, they started their writers' notebooks.

"Sunshine has sharp claws," wrote Buddy. "I named her Sunshine, but she's not sunny. She's more stormy."

He also drew a picture of her. Because Bea was probably right. If you didn't practice drawing, you'd never get better.

Bea hadn't started writing yet. She was making impatient little huffing noises. Like she was having a hard time getting started. She peered over Buddy's shoulder to read what he wrote.

"Why's she have a wrong name?" she asked.

"Because I named her before we knew," said Buddy. "When we got her, I was happy. So my dads said, 'Name her a happy name!' We didn't know yet that she was a biter and scratcher."

"Her name should be Stormy," said Bea.

Buddy shrugged. "You just have to remember. She's the opposite."

Priya leaned across from the next table. She was looking at Joey's page. He was drawing a picture of a dog. "Is that your dog?" she asked.

"Yeah," said Joey.

"Is it a service dog?" asked Priya.

"No," said Joey. "She's just a *dog* dog."

"My uncle trains service dogs," said Priya. "To do stuff."

"What kind of stuff?" asked Joey.

"*Important* stuff," said Priya. "Like save people."

"Wow," said Buddy. Save people? That was impressive.

"Once he trained a dog for a *school*," said Priya.

"To save *kids*?" asked Buddy.

"No," said Priya. "More like a comfort dog. So kids could pet him and feel better."

Bea nodded, as if she understood. "Yeah," she said. "Like if they got yelled at. Or had a time-out."

"Or had to take a big test," said Priya.

"We should get a comfort dog," said Bea. "Could your uncle get us one?"

"I think it's a long, complicated process," said Priya.

"What about just for a day?" asked Joey. "Maybe a dog could visit."

They asked Ms. Maple.

"That's an interesting idea," she said. But she seemed distracted. She'd been peering over their shoulders to see what they were writing. "Are you *all* writing about pets?" she asked.

"Yeah," said Tamar.

"You don't have to, you know," said Ms. Maple.

"We *want* to," said Malik.

"It's our theme now," said Omar.

"Pet-a-Palooza," said Bea. "It's our . . . *ah-Jedi*. Like you said."

"*Agenda*," Tamar corrected her.

"But what if someone doesn't have a pet?" said Ms. Maple. "Maybe some Whirligigs don't."

"Then," said Marisol, "they could write about pigeons. In the park."

"Or a cat in a store," said Malik. "Like a bodega cat."

Buddy nodded. He knew about bodega cats. All the little convenience stores in the city that sold soda and sandwiches had cats living in them. They were a thing!

"I don't have a pet," said Amber. "But I help my neighbors walk their dog. So I can write about that." She pointed to Bea. "And Bea doesn't have a pet, either."

"Yes, I do," said Bea. "A cat. I have a cat."

"You do?" said Amber. "When I came to your house, I didn't see one."

"Because she's shy," said Bea. "With people. *Other* people. Not with me. You didn't see her, but guess what? She saw you. I saw her peeking. From behind the chair."

"Oh," said Amber. "Wow. What's her name?"

There was a long pause. Bea looked around the room. As if she'd forgotten the name and might find it there. "Booky," she said.

"Booky?"

"Yeah, because he likes books."

"'He'?" said Amber. "You said 'she' before."

"No," said Bea. "*You* said 'she.' You must've heard me wrong."

Buddy couldn't remember. *Had* Bea said "she"?

"Well, which is it?" asked Amber.

"He," said Bea. She started drawing in her notebook. A picture of a cat. "It's my cat, so I should know if it's a boy or a girl, shouldn't I?" She held up her drawing. Like a dare. "See?"

CHAPTER FOUR
Herding Cats

It was Marisol's idea to make a chart. During math, she made a chart of how many kids had which pets.

Kaveh had an ant farm. That was a lot of pets! But Marisol only counted it as one.

A lot of Whirligigs had dogs. Marisol put Amber and Priya in that column. Because of Amber's neighbor dog. And Priya's uncle, the guy who was the trainer. Buddy wished he had a dog. He'd give it rides, like Joey gave Frisbee. Maybe on his scooter.

But Buddy was in the cat column, the biggest category. And somehow, everyone's cat sounded better than his. Even Omar's. And his cat had died over the summer. Omar had written a whole sad page in his notebook about the day Mr. Mustard died, and what a great cat he'd been.

Buddy wanted to make Omar feel better. "I could lend you Sunshine," he said. But Omar shook his head and looked teary. "I just miss Mr. Mustard," he said.

Keiko had a cat, too. She'd written a poem about him.

> *At night, when Angel lies*
> *Across my chest,*
> *It feels like my heart crawled out of my body*
> *And started purring.*

Wow. How did Keiko even come up with stuff like that? Keiko's cat sounded *way* better than Sunshine!

Bea stood next to Marisol, stabbing at the cat column. "There," she said. "Put me there." She kept talking about her cat. "Booky likes to sleep on cans." She said it like a brag.

"Cans?" said Keiko.

"Yeah."

"What cans?"

"The ones in my house."

"You mean like *garbage* cans?" asked Malik.

"No. *Cans.* For food."

"Cats don't like to sleep on cans," said Omar. "They like soft things." Then Omar's voice got sad again. "Mr. Mustard liked to sleep on my lap."

Buddy felt sorry for Omar. Really, he did. But he also felt a little jealous. How could Omar's dead cat seem better than his live one? Buddy knew that was kind of weird. To be jealous of a dead cat. But he couldn't help it. Sometimes feelings were weird.

"How come Booky sleeps on cans?" he asked Bea.

"Because I *trained* him to," she said. "Cats love cans. Because of course they do! *Cat* almost sounds like *can*. Only one letter is different!"

The things Bea said about Booky didn't even make sense. Still, she managed to brag about him. Buddy wished he could brag about Sunshine. But there was something about her, something she *did*, that was way worse than biting and scratching. It was super embarrassing! No way could he tell!

But then Buddy got an idea. If Bea had trained her cat, maybe he could train his. Maybe Sunshine could be like a service dog. Except she'd be a service *cat*. She might not be cuddly like other cats. But maybe she could *do* things.

That night at dinner, Buddy told his dads his plan. "I'm going to train Sunshine," he said.

Daddo was in the middle of sipping his water. He spit it right out. That was called a "spit take." Buddy knew that because Daddo was an actor. And actors did spit takes to be funny. On TV and in movies and onstage. But this spit take was real.

Daddo wiped his mouth with his napkin. "You're going to train *Sunshine*?" he asked.

"Why not?" asked Buddy.

"Because Sunshine's, well...she's Sunshine," said Daddo.

"I know she's not cuddly," said Buddy. "But I could train her to do stuff. Cool stuff."

"And how would you do that?" asked Poppy.

"Treats," said Buddy. "I saw it on a show. You give them a treat when they do what you want them to."

"What would you train her to do?" asked Poppy.

"Fetch my slippers," said Buddy. "Or a toy."

"Those are dog tricks," said Daddo. "Not cat tricks."

"But Sunshine's smart," said Buddy. "You always say."

"She is," said Daddo. "But she's cat-smart. Not dog-smart."

"Buddy," said Poppy. "There's an expression. 'Like herding cats.'"

"What does that mean?" asked Buddy.

"It's what people say when they mean something can't be done," said Poppy. "Cats can't be herded. They do what they want to do. Not what *you* want them to."

"Think about it," said Daddo. "Have we *ever* been able to train Sunshine? At all? Not even so she doesn't—"

"Oh no!" said Poppy, cutting him off. "Stop right there. You know the rule! No bathroom talk. Not at the dinner table!"

Daddo winked at Buddy. Because they all knew what he'd been about to say. It was the worst thing about Sunshine. The thing she did that was the absolute most embarrassing.

"Sunshine's a weird cat," said Buddy.

"She is," said Poppy.

"But she's *our* weird cat," said Daddo.

Buddy excused himself from the table. To sneak off to train Sunshine. He knew he could do it. No matter what his dads said.

But in fifteen minutes, he was back.

"Where's the bandages?" he asked. "I can't find them."

"You need a bandage?" said Poppy. "What for?"

Buddy showed them his arm. It was full of scratches.

"Yikes!" said Daddo. Some of the scratches looked deep. "Let me guess. You tried to train Sunshine."

Buddy nodded.

Poppy wet a paper towel. He sudsed it up with soap. Then he dabbed at Buddy's arm to clean all the bloody places.

"Ouch!" said Buddy.

"If you want to train a pet," said Daddo, "train a dog."

"We don't have a dog," said Buddy.

But then he remembered. Joey did.

Maybe he and Joey could train Frisbee.

CHAPTER FIVE
Training Frisbee

The next day after school, Buddy went to Joey's house. They went straight to Joey's bedroom. Buddy told Joey his idea. "I think we should train Frisbee."

"I told you," said Joey. "She's not a service dog."

"It doesn't matter," said Buddy. "You can train *any* dog. You just can't train cats. They won't let you." He showed Joey the scratches on his arm. As proof.

"Wow," said Joey. Buddy's cuts were impressive.

"But Frisbee will learn easy," said Buddy. "Especially since she's still a puppy."

"What would we train her to do?" asked Joey.

"What do you *want* her to do?" asked Buddy.

Joey thought. "I'm not sure," he said.

"Priya's uncle's dog saves people," said Buddy. "So maybe Frisbee could save you."

"How?"

"Like if there's a burglar or something," said Buddy.

"Or an evil villain guy," said Joey. "Sometimes I wake up in the middle of the night and there might be an evil villain guy in the room. But I'm not sure."

Whoa! That had happened to Buddy! Exactly! "I know!" said Buddy. "Right?"

"I turn on my lamp," said Joey. "But the room's still dark. So I always wish I could turn on the *big* light. The overhead one."

"That's it!" said Buddy. "We'll train *Frisbee* to do that!"

"How?" asked Joey.

"We'll give her treats. Do you have treats?"

"Yeah. But I don't think she can reach the light switch. She's too little."

Hmm. That *was* a problem. Frisbee *was* little. An itty-bitty fluffy pup. She definitely wasn't big enough to reach the light switch. Even if she stood on her hind legs.

Buddy thought. "She'll have to stand on a chair." He looked around the room. There wasn't one. Not even at Joey's desk. "Where's the desk chair?" he asked.

Joey pointed to his wheelchair. "This," he said. "This is my chair."

"Oh," said Buddy. "Right." He hadn't thought of that, that Joey didn't need other chairs. "Whoops," he said. "I forgot."

"That's okay," said Joey. "I'll remind you."

"Cool," said Buddy. They bumped fists.

"So what could Frisbee stand on?" asked Buddy.

Joey wheeled out the door, waving Buddy to follow.

Joey lived in a big apartment with a fancy dining room. It had a long table with lots of chairs. Buddy picked one up. He carried it back to Joey's room. Then they went to the kitchen to bring back a bag of dog treats. Now they were all set. All they needed was Frisbee. Where was that pup, anyway?

"Give me the bag," said Joey. "She loves treats. She'll come running."

Joey shook the bag. Frisbee bounded into the bedroom.

"See?" said Buddy. "You already trained her. To come when you call. This'll be easy!"

Buddy patted the chair and called Frisbee. But she didn't come. So Buddy put a treat on the seat. Frisbee just cocked her head, as if she were asking a question. Like, "*What?*"

Buddy picked her up and set her on the chair. Frisbee ate the treat. But then she jumped right down.

"Frisbee!" cried Buddy. "Come back!"

"I'll get her to do it," said Joey. He wheeled close to Frisbee and held out another treat. "Here, Frisbee!" he coaxed. "Treats!"

As Frisbee moved toward him, Joey backed up, wheeling toward the chair. Closer. Closer. He put the treat on the seat. But Frisbee wouldn't jump up.

Buddy grabbed her around her middle. "Up you go, little fuzzy-wuzz!" He lifted her onto the chair again, then tried to nudge her toward the light switch. But Frisbee yelped. She leaped off the chair, right onto Joey's lap.

Hmm. It was hard to train a dog. Harder than Buddy had realized. He tried to pick her up again. Frisbee whined. She buried her head under Joey's arm.

"Joey," said Buddy. "Don't pet her."

"I'm not," said Joey. "She just loves me. I can't help it!"

When Buddy tried to lift her again, Frisbee jumped off Joey's lap. She leaped onto the bed. Buddy lunged to catch her. But Frisbee bounded away, onto the bedside table.

Uh-oh! She knocked into the lamp. It teetered.

Buddy caught the lamp before it crashed to the floor. But Frisbee had already knocked over some other things. A stack of books. And a glass of water.

"Hey!" It was Joey's mom. She was in the doorway. She'd heard the noise. "What's going on?" She looked at the glass. And the water on the floor.

"We were trying to train Frisbee," said Joey. "But she didn't want to learn."

"Train her to do what?" asked his mom.

"Turn on the light in the middle of the night," said Joey.

"In case there's an evil villain guy," said Buddy.

Joey's mom made a face. Like she didn't believe them. Probably she didn't know about evil villain guys. Maybe she hadn't watched the same shows. She picked up the glass and set it back on the table. She blotted up the water with her dish towel.

"Do you guys want a snack?" she asked.

They did! And Frisbee, too! In the kitchen, Joey's mom made apple slices with peanut butter. Frisbee loved the peanut butter part. She licked some off Joey's apple. Then she gave Joey a slurpy kiss. Because his lips had gotten a little peanut buttery, too.

"Hey!" said Buddy. "I want a kiss!"

He leaned over and pursed his lips. Frisbee slurped at them. Her tongue was tickly!

"See?" said Buddy. "We did train her."

"Maybe she just doesn't want to turn on the light," said Joey.

"And see an evil villain guy," said Buddy. Who could blame her? "But she's a really good comfort dog. As good as Priya's uncle's dogs, I bet."

"Yeah," said Joey. He rested his chin on Frisbee's head. "Frisbee, you'd make every kid at school feel better. Wouldn't you?"

Joey's mom sat down with them at the table. "Do they allow dogs at school?" she asked.

"Maybe," said Joey. "Like, maybe for a visit."

Frisbee wagged her tail. Then she put her puppy paws on the table. And licked the rest of the peanut butter off the plate.

CHAPTER SIX
Fuzzy

The next morning, when they got to school, Buddy and Joey told everybody about training Frisbee. They didn't mention the part about the light switch.

"We trained her to lick peanut butter!" said Joey.

"Peanut butter?" scoffed Priya. "Any dog will eat that."

"Yeah," said Bea. "I trained Booky to do stuff that's much harder."

Buddy hung his baseball cap in his cubby. "No way," he said. "You can't train cats." He thought of Sunshine. "Unless you want to train them to scratch you all up."

Oops. Buddy hadn't meant to say that. He didn't want to call attention to his scratches. He'd even worn long sleeves to cover them. Bea noticed.

"Do *you* have scratches?" she asked.

"No."

Bea tugged up his sleeve. Her mouth gaped open. "Did *Sunshine* do that?" She touched a cut.

"Ouch!" said Buddy.

"We need to wash these," said Bea. "Right away! They're *oozing*!"

"That's *ointment*!" said Buddy.

"Oh." Bea wiped her goopy finger on his shirt. Yuck! "Well," she said, "at least you don't need stitches. Trust me. I know. I'm an *expert* on stitches. So you're lucky I'm here to help."

Not really, thought Buddy.

He headed to morning meeting.

On the rug, the Whirligigs took turns reading from their writers' notebooks. When it was Bea's turn, she smoothed the page. She took a deep breath. "My cat is cute," she read. Then she looked up and smiled.

"Bea," said Ms. Maple. "Can you add more specific detail? That might help us imagine your cat more clearly. Whirligigs, can you think of any questions to ask Bea? To help her out?"

"Like, *how* is he cute, exactly?" asked Omar.

"He's *super* cute," said Bea.

Omar made a face. "That sounds kind of fuzzy."

"Yeah," said Keiko. "Maybe you could *say* he's fuzzy. And that would sound *less* fuzzy."

Ms. Maple split them into pairs to go back to their tables. "Your job," she said, "is to help each other add detail. *Sensory* detail. Ask your partner: How did something feel? And smell?"

Buddy wanted to work with Joey. So they could talk about Frisbee. About how her tongue felt tickly. And how she smelled like peanut butter.

But Ms. Maple paired him with Bea. Bea dragged him to their table. She opened her notebook and read the same thing she'd read before. "My cat is cute."

Buddy let out a frustrated breath. Working with Bea was the hardest job in the class!

"Did you even *hear* Ms. Maple?" he asked. "You're supposed to be *specific*. How *exactly* is he cute? You need to tell. You need to say *detail*." Buddy almost smiled. Because it felt kind of fun being the teacher. Bossing Bea around.

"All right," said Bea. She scrunched her face, thinking. Then she wrote something else. "My cat is wonderful," she read.

"*Wonderful?*" said Buddy. "That's not more specific. It's not any better than *cute*."

"Yes, it is," said Bea. "It's a bigger word."

"No!" said Buddy. "Use words that *show* something. Like *soft*. Or *striped*. Or *puffy tail*."

Bea scowled. "I don't like those words," she said. "I already said my words. *Cute* and *wonderful*. That's plenty. In fact, I'm done with words. Pictures are better. A picture is worth *a thousand* words. Did you ever hear that? I'll draw a picture. Because I'm a good *illustrator*."

Then Bea turned away and started drawing.

This was impossible! Buddy couldn't make Bea do anything. It was like herding cats!

Bea slid her notebook toward him. She'd drawn another picture of a cat. The cat was sprawled across a really long shelf. The shelf was crammed with something. What? Buddy couldn't tell.

"What's that?" he asked, pointing.

Bea made a face. "*Cans*," she said. "I *told* you."

"But," said Buddy, "why are there so many?"

"For *food*. My gran *cooks* with them."

Across the aisle, Omar leaned over. He wanted to see, too.

"That looks like a shelf in a store," he said. His face was puckered. Like he was trying to figure it out. "Like the bodega on my corner."

"Hey, Bea!" Malik joined in. "Is your cat a *bodega* cat?"

"Booky the Bodega Cat!" said Kaveh. "He guards the shelves!"

"From all the bodega mice!" said Malik.

Bea made a face at them. Like she didn't care. Though obviously she did. "I was going to tell you all something," she said. "Something *I* know but you don't. But I'm not telling now." She went back to her drawing, making a big show of shading in the cans. And then she started singing! A bouncy, goofy, nonsense song.

Doopity-doopity-doopity-doo
Doop-doop-dee-diddle-ee-doo!

What was she singing? It wasn't even a song! Bea could be so annoying!

Buddy knew he should probably start writing in his own notebook. But how could he concentrate? Bea was acting too weird!

Even weirder than usual!

CHAPTER SEVEN
Fibber

At recess, Buddy waited outside for Joey. *All* the Whirligigs were waiting. During lunch, Joey had told them he'd made up a new game. But just as they'd been heading out to play, Ms. Maple had come to the cafeteria. She'd called Joey aside to talk to him. Now, outside, Buddy kept staring at the door. Where was Joey? Why wasn't he coming?

Oh. There he was!

Everyone crowded around Joey as he explained his game. They needed a ball. And two teams. Dogs versus Cats. Since a lot more Whirligigs had cats, Joey put all the kids with other pets onto Team Dog.

Buddy and Bea were both Team Cat. But Buddy got knocked out of the game early on. Because the rules were a little confusing. When the ball came his way, was he supposed to catch it? Or throw it back? He hadn't listened very carefully.

In a few minutes, Bea joined him on the sidelines. And other kids, too, as they got eliminated one by one. Bea started jabbering on again about her cat.

"He doesn't just sleep on cans," Bea was saying. "Sometimes crates. He tests out every crate in the pile."

"You have a *pile* of crates?" asked Marisol. "At *home*? Why?"

"Because Booky *likes* them."

Bea leaned away from Marisol, toward Buddy. She cupped her hand around his ear, like she was whispering. Only she wasn't whispering. She was talking loudly, like she wanted everyone to hear. "Remember I said I *know* something? Something you *don't*?"

"Yeah?" said Buddy.

"Well, guess what? I ran into somebody! Yesterday. After school."

"Who?" asked Buddy.

"Guess," said Bea.

Bea loved to play "Guess." But Buddy hated it. It could be endless.

"No," he said. "I'm not guessing."

"Hey, everybody," said Bea. She waved the others close. "Guess who I saw?" She paused. "Yesterday after school?" No one guessed. "Roxy Fox!" she cried. "I ran into her! The *author*!"

"You did not," said Priya.

"Did too," said Bea.

"Where?" asked Marisol.

"Guess!" said Bea.

"No!" cried Buddy.

But Tamar guessed, "The library." Because that would make sense.

"Nope."

"The bookstore," tried Keiko. Because that would make sense, too.

Bea shook her head again.

"Tell us already!" said Buddy.

"The store," said Bea.

"Which store?" asked Keiko.

"The little store," said Bea. "On the big street. Where Gran buys milk."

"I don't believe you," said Tamar.

Bea's eyes flashed. "Are you saying I'm *a liar*?"

"Well," said Tamar, "maybe not a *full-out* liar. But maybe just a *little*. Like a *fibber*."

Bea grabbed Amber's arm. "Amber knows I'm telling the truth. Don't you, Amber?"

Amber looked squirmy. Like Bea had shined a spotlight on her, and she didn't want to be in it. Bea clutched her arm tighter.

"Come on!" said Bea. "You're my best friend!"

"Well," Amber said carefully. "I wasn't actually *there* with you."

Omar squinted at Bea. "Wait," he said. "*Have* you been fibbing? All along? About *everything*? Like about your cat?"

"*NO!*"

"Because it occurred to me," he said. "Maybe your cat is imaginary. Like an imaginary friend. But an imaginary *cat*."

"Do you really have a cat?" asked Malik.

"I do!" said Bea. "Booksy!"

"I thought his name was Booky," said Kaveh.

"I changed it!" said Bea.

"You can't just change your cat's name," said Marisol.

"It's *my* cat," said Bea. "I can do whatever I want!"

No one knew what to say to Bea. They shook their heads and rolled their eyes. Joey was calling them back to play another round of the game.

"Amber!" cried Bea. "Don't go!" But Amber ran off with the others.

Buddy was the only one who stayed behind. He couldn't stop staring at Bea.

Did Bea have an imaginary cat? And an *imaginary author*, too?

Is this what a fibber looks like? he wondered.

"I'm not a fibber," muttered Bea. Wow. Had she known what he was thinking? Was Bea *a mind reader*? "I really did see Roxy Fox."

"Oh yeah?" said Buddy. "Prove it."

"How?" said Bea.

Buddy thought. What had Ms. Maple told them to do? "Tell more *detail*!" he said.

"Like what?" said Bea.

"I don't know," said Buddy. "Like, what did she *buy* there?" Oh ho! Bea couldn't wriggle away now! She couldn't just keep fibbing forever!

Bea grinned. A snaky, crooked grin. "Guess," she said.

"*NO!!!!*" cried Buddy.

"Buddy!" called Joey. "Come on!"

Buddy stood up. "Are you coming?" he asked.

Bea reached toward him. Was she trying to take his hand? No. She leaned around behind him and slapped at the seat of his pants.

"Hey!" cried Buddy. He jumped clear.

"You've got dirt," said Bea. "On your can."

"On my *can*?" said Buddy.

"*Can* means *butt*," said Bea. "That's what Gran calls it."

"Stop saying *can!*" cried Buddy.

Bea crossed her arms. "I'll say whatever I want. And I *do* have a cat. He's not imaginary. He's cute. And wonderful."

Every time Bea talked about her cat, it sounded weird, all wrong. It didn't sound like a cat. It sounded *fishy*!

"Buddy!" Joey called again. "We're starting!"

Buddy ran off to join the game. He left Bea sitting there.

Alone.

And sulking.

CHAPTER EIGHT
Dog for a Day

After recess, Ms. Maple said she had a treat for the class.

"Is it cake?" asked Omar.

"No."

"Pizza?" asked Malik.

"Not food," said Ms. Maple.

Buddy groaned. "Not another author visit!" He looked at Joey and rolled his eyes. But Joey was grinning wildly.

"Joey," said Ms. Maple. "Would you like to tell the class what we arranged?"

"Frisbee!" he cried. "Frisbee's coming to visit!" Whoa! "My mom's bringing her! Right now! She can be our Dog for a Day! Our *comfort* dog!"

Ms. Maple let Joey and Buddy go to the front entrance to wait for them. They stood near the safety-agent desk with Ms. King. When they told her that Frisbee was coming, she raised an eyebrow.

"Now, you know I can't allow any dog inside here," she said. Was she teasing? Sometimes Ms. King liked to tease. "I can't have animals in my school. Or any trouble like that."

Was she serious? Hard to tell.

"Frisbee!" cried Joey. Frisbee burst through the door, straining at her leash. She was so excited, she yanked the leash from Joey's mom. Then she bolted past Ms. King and down the hall, running straight into the principal. She zoomed round and round, tangling the leash between Ms. Flores's ankles. Joey and Buddy tried to unwind it.

"Sorry," said Joey. "She's just excited."

"No worries," said Ms. Flores. "I'm excited, too. I was just coming to join your class!"

Inside the classroom, the Whirligigs jumped up from the rug. They clustered around Frisbee as soon as she ran through the door.

At first, they all tried to pet her at once, in one big crush. Then they tried one at a time. But that took too long.

So Ms. Maple organized them into small groups, to pet Frisbee together. When they'd finished, Ms. Maple said they could ask Joey questions about her. But everyone just wanted to pet Frisbee. So they started all over.

Frisbee loved the attention. Her tail wagged wildly. But when the second round of petting started, she wriggled free and raced to the cubbies. She wrestled out a bag there. It had somebody's snack inside. Not for long! Frisbee ate it!

Then she grabbed a boot out of the next cubby.

"Sit!" Joey said firmly. "Stay!"

But Frisbee ran to Joey with the boot in her mouth. She dropped it in front of him like a gift. Then she jumped up on her hind legs. As if she were a circus dog doing a trick!

Priya frowned. "I thought you said you trained her."

"We did," said Joey. "To eat peanut butter! We didn't train her for other stuff. But she's a really good comfort dog."

Priya nuzzled Frisbee. "She is," she agreed. "She's so soft."

Bea sidled up next to Frisbee, edging Priya aside. "I need *special* comfort," she said. She laced her arms around Frisbee's neck. "Because everyone called me a fibber. But I'm *not*."

Frisbee whined, as if she felt sorry for Bea. Then she lapped at Bea's lips, a wet, sloppy dog kiss. And Frisbee and Bea stayed that way, laced together in a comfort hug for a very long time. Until suddenly...

Frisbee dashed away. She squatted on the floor.

"Frisbee!" cried Joey. "Don't!"

But she did.

Buddy could hardly believe it.

"She piddled," said Amber.

"In a puddle," said Keiko.

She'd peed!

Everyone laughed. And laughed and laughed. No one could stop.

Ms. Maple grabbed a roll of paper towels and a soapy cleanser and helped Joey's mom clean up the "accident."

"I think Frisbee needs a walk," said Joey's mom. "I'll drop her at home before pickup."

The Whirligigs jammed together at the door to wave goodbye. Once Frisbee left, Ms. Maple said they could take out their writers' notebooks.

They had plenty to write about now. Thanks to Frisbee!

Buddy sucked on the end of his pencil, thinking. He'd noticed something during Frisbee's visit. Something interesting. No one seemed to mind that Frisbee had peed on the floor. They thought it was funny. Cute, even.

That made Buddy wonder. Should he tell about Sunshine? Should he write the thing he swore he'd never reveal?

Buddy bent over his notebook. When it was time to share entries, he raised his hand.

"There's something about my cat Sunshine that I've never told," he read. He looked around to make sure the others were listening. They were. "She plays with her poop."

"*Ewwww!*" cried everyone. Though their eyes were wide and expectant. Glistening, even! Did they want more?

"Sometimes," Buddy continued, "we think she's playing with a toy. But then we look closer. And it's not. It's poop! A little ball of it! She paws a dry one out of her litter box. And bats it around the house."

"Epic!" said Kaveh.

"My dude!" said Omar.

Malik fist-bumped him.

"Now *that's* detail!" said Joey.

"It's definitely detail," said Ms. Maple. "I think we were all able to see what you described. Very vividly."

"And smell it, too!" said Joey.

CHAPTER NINE
Bodega Cat

Ms. Maple had taken a lot of photos during Frisbee's visit. She scrolled through her tablet to show the class. The tablet *binged*.

"Oh," she said. "An email. From Roxy." She clicked it open. "Hey! It's for you all!" She read it aloud.

> Hi, Whirligigs! How are your notebooks coming? I was so glad to hear about them when I ran into Bea.

Buddy gasped. Wait. What? Bea was in the *email*? "See!" said Bea. "I told you! I *did* run into Roxy Fox!" Ms. Maple kept reading.

Bea and I observed the cat at the store. He was napping, sprawled across a low shelf. Bea told me she'd trained him to lie there so she could sit on a crate and pet him.

"So," said Amber. "You actually *were* writing about a cat at the store? A cat that *lives there*?"

"You were writing about *a bodega cat*?" said Omar.

Bea made an *Eeek!* face. Like she'd been caught.

"Ha!" said Malik. "I knew it! I told you!"

"You *did* fib!" said Tamar.

"I never said the cat lived with me," said Bea.

"You said it was *yours*," said Amber.

"Because it *could* be," said Bea. "It could be anybody's. A bodega cat can belong to everyone."

"No, it can't," said Buddy. "It belongs to *the bodega*."

"No," said Bea. "Like for instance. You might think the cookies on the shelves there belong to the store. But *then*, they belong to the person who brings them home. See?"

"Because they *bought* them," said Buddy.

"You're not *listening* to me!" said Bea.

"Because you're not making sense!" said Buddy. Sometimes Bea's thinking was twisty as a pretzel!

Ms. Maple quieted the class. "So, Bea," she said. "You didn't have a pet at home to write about. Is that right?"

Bea hung her head. And looked away. "Mm-hmm," she admitted. Just barely.

Buddy hoped Ms. Maple would lecture Bea. He wanted her to tell Bea it wasn't good to fib. That fibbing was just as bad as lying. Because it really was!

"Well," said Ms. Maple. "I think you came up with a creative solution."

Bea's head snapped up. "I did?"

"You didn't have a pet at home," said Ms. Maple. "So you found a cat you could observe."

"I did," said Bea.

"It took extra effort," said Ms. Maple. "Many Whirligigs could observe pets at home. But you had to search one out."

"Yeah," said Bea. "And if people thought my pet lived at home? That wasn't fibbing. It was *fiction*. *Roxy Fox* writes fiction. And she taught us. So I *learned*!"

"Well," said Ms. Maple, "I do hope all the Whirligigs in this class tell the truth."

"Me, too," said Bea. She stared at everyone. Everyone *else*. "You should *all* tell the truth. And stop telling lies. Like saying I'm a *fibber*!"

Buddy caught his breath. Would Ms. Maple *punish* Bea? For *blaming*? On top of *lying*? Somebody had to set Bea straight!

"Actually, Bea," said Ms. Maple. "There's a difference between writing fiction and having a conversation in real life. When we're talking with our classmates, they should be able to expect that we're telling the truth. That's important for our Whirligig community. Can you agree?"

Bea looked away. She murmured something, though Buddy couldn't quite hear. Had she said yes?

Ms. Maple looked back at her tablet. "Oh," she said. "We never finished Roxy's email. You're going to like this last part." She read the rest aloud.

> Seeing the bodega cat made me wish I had a pet. So I went to the animal shelter and adopted one! He's a tabby cat with a big swirl on his side. I named him Whirligig. After you all, because you inspired me!

"Wow!" said Priya. "We inspired her!"

"I'm not surprised," said Ms. Maple. "You Whirligigs can be very inspiring."

"Our *pets* are inspiring," said Keiko.

"Especially Lotto," said Bea.

"Lotto?" asked Ms. Maple.

"The bodega cat," said Bea. "His name's not Booky. Or Booksy. It's Lotto. 'Cause they sell lottery tickets there. My gran likes to play those scratch-off games. She gives me a quarter. To do the scratching-off part. You do it with the edge. Like this." She mimed scraping the numbers clean on the ticket. She scrunched her face, concentrating hard.

"My dad plays those games," said Marisol. "But he doesn't win much."

"Well, *I* win," said Bea. "Every time! Because Gran forgets she gave me the quarter. So I get to keep it!"

The tablet *binged* again. Ms. Maple smiled, then panned it in front of the class so they could see, too.

It was a photo. Of Roxy Fox's swirly new cat.

Everyone cooed. "*Awwww!*"

Underneath, Roxy had typed one word.

          Pet-a-Palooza!

"Hey," said Bea. "That reminds me. I have a question I've been wondering this whole long time. What *is* a palooza, anyway?"

"It's a big party," said Ms. Maple. "With a lot of one specific thing."

"Like pets?" asked Bea.

"Exactly," said Ms. Maple.

Bea slumped. She looked wilted. "You know what?" she said. "I think I've had enough of pets for a while."

Buddy knew what she meant. He felt a little wilty himself. Thinking about pets all day long could be exhausting.

"Next time we have a big palooza?" said Bea. "How about we just have a lot of cake."

"Chocolate!" cried Buddy. "No! Vanilla! Wait! *All* the kinds!"

Bea grinned at Buddy. She bobbed her head yes.

"A *Cake-a-*Palooza!" she said.

Sweet!

ACKNOWLEDGMENTS

It takes a lot of people to turn a manuscript into a book. Once I finish writing, Kris, the illustrator, sets to work creating the really fun art you see on the cover and inside pages. But behind the scenes, there are also lots of people helping the books. Thanks to my agent, Andrea; Catherine, the editor; Lily, the designer; Jamie, the copy editor; plus Terry, Sara, and all the great folks on the Marketing & Publicity team.

It was Catherine, the editor, for example, who suggested I add a chapter in which Frisbee actually visits the classroom.

Frisbee, no! Don't!

Oops. Too late. Frisbee piddled!

Thanks also to our Kid Consultants, my niece Phoebe and Catherine's son William.

And there were many people over many years who *inspired* these stories: all the kids I met when I was a teacher and when my son was in school, plus all the top-notch teachers I've met along the way.

TRUE OR FALSE?

In this book, Sunshine does worse than piddle. She plays with dried-up balls of poo from her litter box. Do I know a cat who actually did that?

TRUE! I do!

It was my own cat, Sadie. She's a weird cat. "But," as Daddo would say, "she's *our* weird cat." So we love her anyway!

ABOUT THE CREATORS

Jan Carr is the author of more than fifty books, including picture books and books in popular series. She has worked as a Head Start teacher, a book editor, a magazine editor at Sesame Workshop, and taught writing at the New School and School of Visual Arts. She lives in New York City with her family, including her cat, Sadie, who is indeed "cute" and "wonderful," but who is also furry, fuzzy, feisty, fearless, and very quirky! Sadie likes to run along the pipes on the ceiling and bathe herself in water (a few inches) in the bathtub. Visit Jan at *JanCarr.net*.

Kris Mukai is a cartoonist and writer who lives and works in Los Angeles. She has drawn illustrations for the *New Yorker* and the *New York Times*. She currently works as a writer at Cartoon Network and has written for *Adventure Time*, *Craig of the Creek*, *We Bare Bears*, and the *WBB* spin-off *We Baby Bears*. In her spare time, she monitors hawk nests in her neighborhood. See more of Kris's work at *HiKrisMukai.com*.

Check out **ALL** of **BUDDY AND BEA'S** adventures!

ISBN: 978-1-68263-534-6

ISBN: 978-1-68263-535-3

ISBN: 978-1-68263-536-0